PETER, THE KNIGHT with ASTHMA

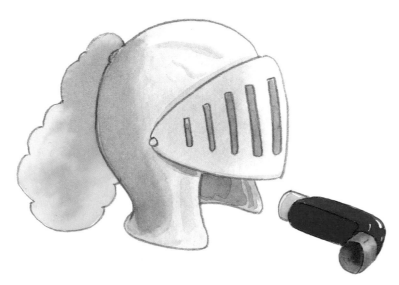

Janna Matthies   Illustrated by Anthony Lewis

Albert Whitman & Company, Morton Grove, Illinois

It is I, Brave Peter, noble knight and protector of the castle. I stand ready, on the lookout for enemies.

Aha! Just as I expected. Out of the woods creeps a ferocious beast! I leap to the ground and charge over hill and stream. "You won't escape this time!" I call.

But wait . . .

Something squeezes my chest. *Cough, cough. Wheeze, wheeze. Sputter, sputter.* "Mom . . . !"

My Lady rushes in with Puffy, my rescue inhaler. "Breathe, Peter!" she says.
I breathe in the medicine and wait to feel better.

"The dragon got away . . ." I tell her, " . . . for the third time this week."
She gives me another puff on the inhaler and says, "Brave Peter, I think it's time
we visit the doctor."

"So Peter," the doctor says the next day, "I hear you've been chasing dragons." I nod. He listens to my chest, then holds something in front of my mouth. "This is a peak flow meter. Blow into it like a fire-breathing dragon."

I blow with all my strength. *Cough, cough. Wheeze, wheeze. Sputter, sputter.* The doctor looks at the meter and back at me. "Pretty good, but let's make you even stronger than a dragon."

The doctor picks up a pen and notepad. "Tell me," he begins, "do these attacks come often?"

"Oh, yes," I say. "The dragon always hides nearby, waiting to catch me by surprise . . ."

"I meant the attacks of coughing and wheezing," he says.

"Oh, right." I sit up straight on the exam table. "Well, there was the time I built an igloo . . . that day we biked through the jungle . . . and the weekend we babysat the tiger cub." My mom fills in the details.

"OK," the doctor says. "Last time a virus was making you cough and wheeze, so we gave you an inhaler. Since then cold weather, cats, and exercise have caused the same trouble. With these new clues, you've led me right to our culprit. Peter . . . you have asthma."

Asthma! My mom and I look at each other. Her eyes seem to say, "Stay brave, Peter!"

"Here's the good news." The doctor smiles. "Now that we can name the beast, we can also tame the beast."

I like the sound of that.

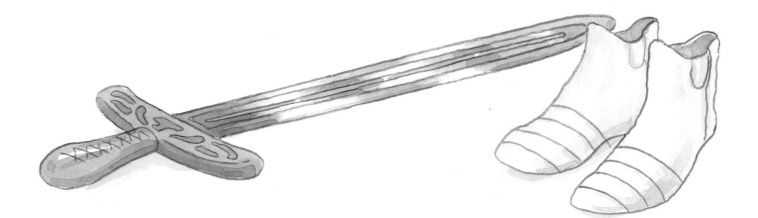

The doctor says I need two new medicines—one to drink for just a few days and another that I'll breathe in every day from now on. I choose a really cool mask, and the nurse shows me how to breathe medicine with a nebulizer machine. She says if I use the nebulizer every day, my lungs will get stronger—which means more time chasing dragons and less time reaching for Puffy.

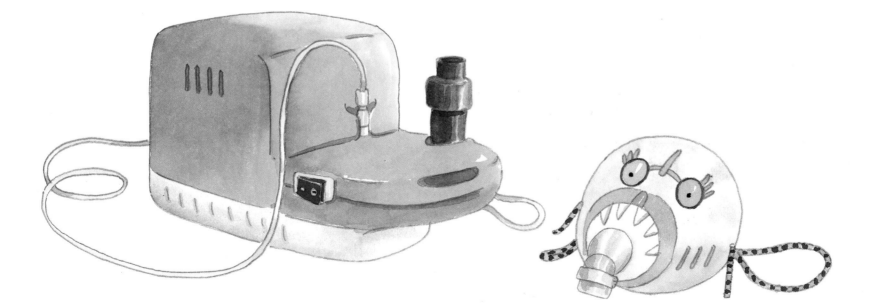

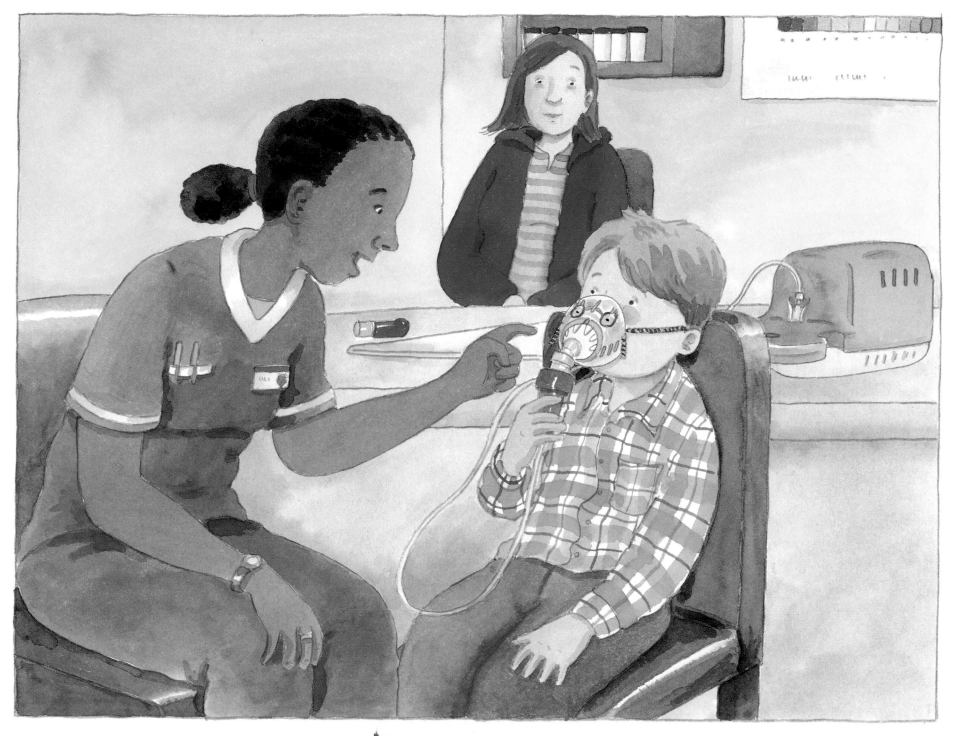

It is I, Brave Peter, Noble Knight of the Nebulizer. I stand ready, keeping watch over my kingdom. All is quiet in the land.

But wait! What's this?

The dragon races out of the woods, thinking I'm gone for good. I leap to the ground and charge over hill and stream. "Ha-ha! Brave Peter is back!" I call. Before he can breathe his smelly fire, I roar louder than any dragon he's ever heard.

Back in my lookout, I watch his tail disappear
into the woods. "Farewell, Dragon-breath!" I call.
But wait . . .

Up from the deep comes a slithering sea monster!
Never fear. I, Brave Peter, will tame the beast!

A Note to Parents

In the United States, asthma causes more "sick child" doctor visits and school absences than any other illness. Every day, thousands of children go to the emergency room and are hospitalized due to asthma. Many of these children require intensive care because of their critical condition. This is a scenario that can and must be avoided.

The good news is that with proper treatment, children and their parents need not fear asthma. Current treatment options make it possible for kids with asthma to live normal, healthy lives without limiting their activities, including playing sports.

There are two main categories of asthma: 1) asthma triggered by external factors like cold viruses, exercise, cigarette smoke, and cold air; and 2) asthma triggered by an allergy to dust, pollens, pet dander, or other allergens. An *asthma attack* can occur when a trigger causes bronchial tubes to constrict and fill with extra mucus, making breathing difficult. While the cause of the disease is unknown, we do know that asthma is inherited; the combination of having it "in your genes" and being exposed to triggers leads to symptoms.

You should consult your family doctor or pediatrician if your child experiences any of these asthma-like symptoms:

+ a cough severe enough to interrupt sleep or exercise
+ wheezing, shortness of breath, or labored breathing with minimal exertion or at rest
+ a simple head cold that lingers for an unusually long time
+ a recurrent diagnosis of bronchitis or pneumonia

Asthma-related doctor exams include questions about symptoms, pattern of attacks (day vs. night, seasonal, exercise-related), family history, and environmental factors (pets in the home,

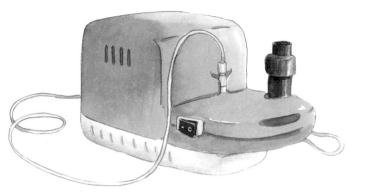

flooded basement, wooded lot, tobacco use). Your doctor will listen to your child's breathing through a stethoscope. And for children five and older, a *peak flow meter* or *pulmonary function test* may be used to measure the child's ability to blow a forceful breath.

If needed, your doctor will prescribe safe, effective and easy-to-use medication. Asthma treatments are either preventive or rescue. The most common and effective preventive treatment is inhaled steroids, breathed in as a mist using a *nebulizer* or as a powder through a hand-held *inhaler.* Inhaled steroids are safe because the lung is the only organ affected. If preventive treatment is used daily, rescue treatment should rarely be needed.

The most common rescue treatment is fast-acting albuterol, taken via inhaler or nebulizer. During an extreme episode, your doctor may also prescribe a few days of oral steroid. However, too much reliance on rescue treatment is a sign of asthma out of control.

Finally, asthma cannot be cured, but it is easy to control. With the help of your doctor, you and your child can keep that pesky dragon at bay.

Michael Tsangaris, M.D.
Associate Professor of Clinical Pediatrics
Indiana University School of Medicine;
Pediatric Pulmonologist
James Whitcomb Riley Hospital
    for Children, Indianapolis, Indiana

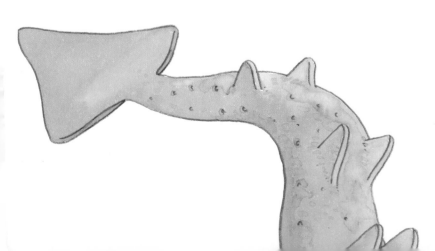

For Jim, Isabelle, Nathan, and Ben—who are all keeping the upper hand on asthma. And with special thanks to Dr. Michael Tsangaris and Dr. Kellie Hughes.—J.M.

For Stephen and Kate.—A.L.

Library of Congress Cataloging-in-Publication Data

Matthies, Janna.
Peter, the knight with asthma / by Janna Matthies ; illustrated by Anthony Lewis.
p. cm.
Summary: When he begins to cough and wheeze while pretending he is a knight slaying dragons,
Peter is taken to the doctor and learns he has asthma and what he can do to control its symptoms.
ISBN 978-0-8075-6517-9
[1. Asthma—Fiction.] I. Lewis, Anthony, 1966- ill. II. Title.
PZ7.M4352Pe 2009 [E—dc22] 2008055694

Text copyright © 2009 by Janna Matthies. Illustrations copyright © 2009 by Anthony Lewis.
Published in 2009 by Albert Whitman & Company, 6340 Oakton Street, Morton Grove, Illinois 60053-2723.
Printed in China.
10 9 8 7 6 5 4 3 2 1

The design is by Carol Gildar.

For more information about Albert Whitman & Company, please visit our web site at www.albertwhitman.com.